The
JUNIOR DISEASE DETECTIVES

DETECTIVES

OPERATION: OUTBREAK

The
JUNI⚲R DISEASE
DETECTIVES
OPERATION: OUTBREAK

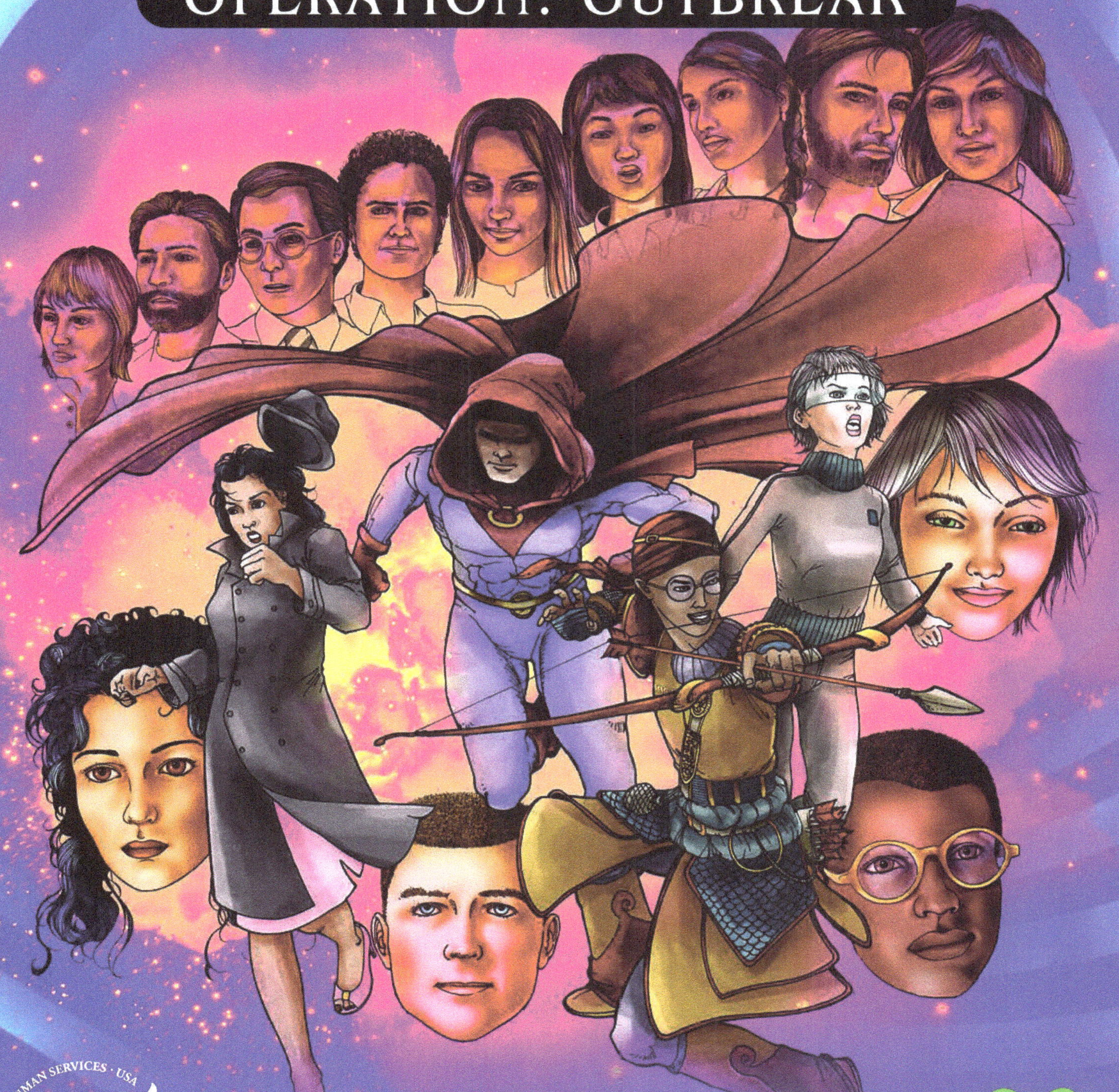

ISBN 978-1-4341-0530-1

This book is made available in electronic form by the CDC, the Centers for Disease Control and Prevention, a United States federal agency:

https://www.cdc.gov

As a U.S. government publication, this book is in the public domain. This printed edition is published by Waking Lion Press, an imprint of the Editorium. Waking Lion Press is not endorsed by or affiliated in any way with the CDC.

Waking Lion Press™ and Editorium™ are trademarks of:

The Editorium, LLC
West Jordan, UT 84081-6132
www.editorium.com

Foreword

The following story is a work of fiction, but real public health threats and diseases are presented. CDC hopes that this story raises youth awareness of infectious diseases and the public health risks they pose. In addition, CDC hopes that this story helps to encourage youth interest in the many different career paths available in public health at the local, state and federal levels. Lastly, CDC hopes that this story promotes youth education and interest in science and public health. We at CDC hope that readers are inspired to become the next generation of real life disease detectives and public health superheroes.

This graphic novel is the result of a partnership between the Centers for Disease Control and Prevention (CDC), 4-H, and the U.S. Department of Agriculture (USDA). 4-H is the nation's largest youth development program. 4-H is a public-private partnership with federal, state, local and non-profit support. Youth and their families access 4-H programs at a community or county level through the cooperative extension division of their land-grant university. 4-H offers a youth development experience for all youth ages 5–19. For more information, please see https://nifa/usda/gov/program/4-h-positive-youth-development.

OPERATION OUTBREAK

PROJECT LEAD: DOUGLAS JORDAN, MA
ART TEAM LEAD: JAMES ARCHER, MSMI
WRITTEN BY DOUGLAS JORDAN, MA
& VICTORIA JEISY SCOTT, PHD
PENCILED & INKED BY BOB HOBBS, AS
DIGITAL COLOR BY KRISTEN IMMOOR, BFA
LETTERING & LAYOUT BY MARK CONNER, BFA
& MEREDITH BOYTER NEWLOVE, MSMI

I HAVE AN *IDEA* TO MAKE THINGS *INTERESTING!* LET'S EACH *IMAGINE* THAT WE ARE FACING A MAJOR *PUBLIC HEALTH THREAT* AND WE ARE THE *HEROES.* EDDIE, LET'S START WITH YOU!

HMM... OK. WELL, I'M PICTURING AN *OUTBREAK* OF A NEW *SCARY DISEASE* THAT HAS ALREADY INFECTED HALF OF THE CITY'S *POPULATION!*

...AND I'M *GERM SLAYER.* THE GERM-FIGHTING *SUPERHERO* WHO HAS THE *CURE!*

I'M THE ONLY HOPE TO DELIVER IT ON TIME!

I REMAIN *CLOAKED* TO MOVE QUICKLY *UNNOTICED* ... I CAN'T RISK BEING *STOPPED* OR *SLOWED DOWN.*

Hospitals and clinics are currently overwhelmed and in some cases people are actually being turned away...

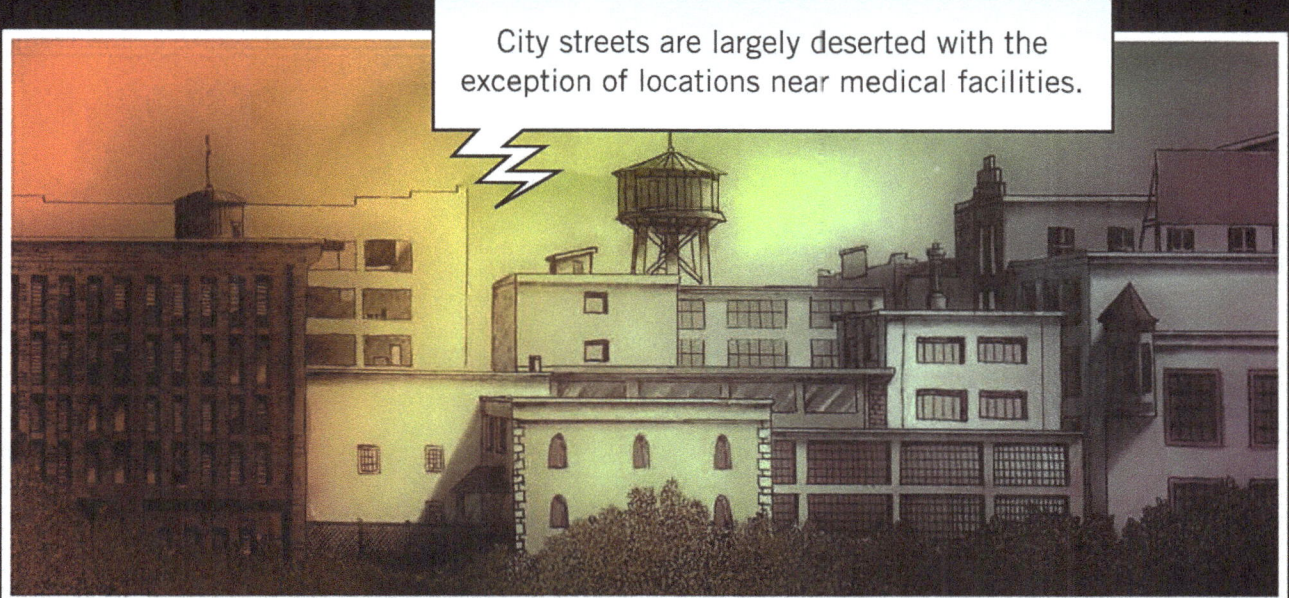

City streets are largely deserted with the exception of locations near medical facilities.

Outside, an army of monster **germs** is **attacking**...

Every germ is different. To **combat** this, a special platoon of i**mmune cells** will be trained to have **defenses** specific to each **germ invader**.

When you get an **infection,** your body **learns** everything it can about the **germ** that causes the **disease.** Your **body's cells** will **remember** what that **specific germ** looks like.

Your **immune cells** are constantly on the lookout for **invading germs**.

When **germs** are spotted and **recognized** by the **immune system,** we must leap into action to **fight** the **infection!**

"The space station is full of people **infected** with an **alien virus,** but I am completely unaware."

"I am just going about my **business.** Little do I know that the space station is **contaminated** with the **virus.** Just by being in the environment, I'm being **exposed** to the **virus!**"

"If you are in a **contaminated environment** and don't take the **proper precautions,** you can get **sick,** too."

"The **virus** can enter a person's eyes, nose or mouth to cause **infection.**"

"Oh no! The **virus** has gotten to **me.** It's trying to **infect me!**"

"**However,** I know that I'll be **safe** because I have been **vaccinated.** **Vaccines** work by causing your **immune system** to recognize and **fight** against the **attacking virus.**"

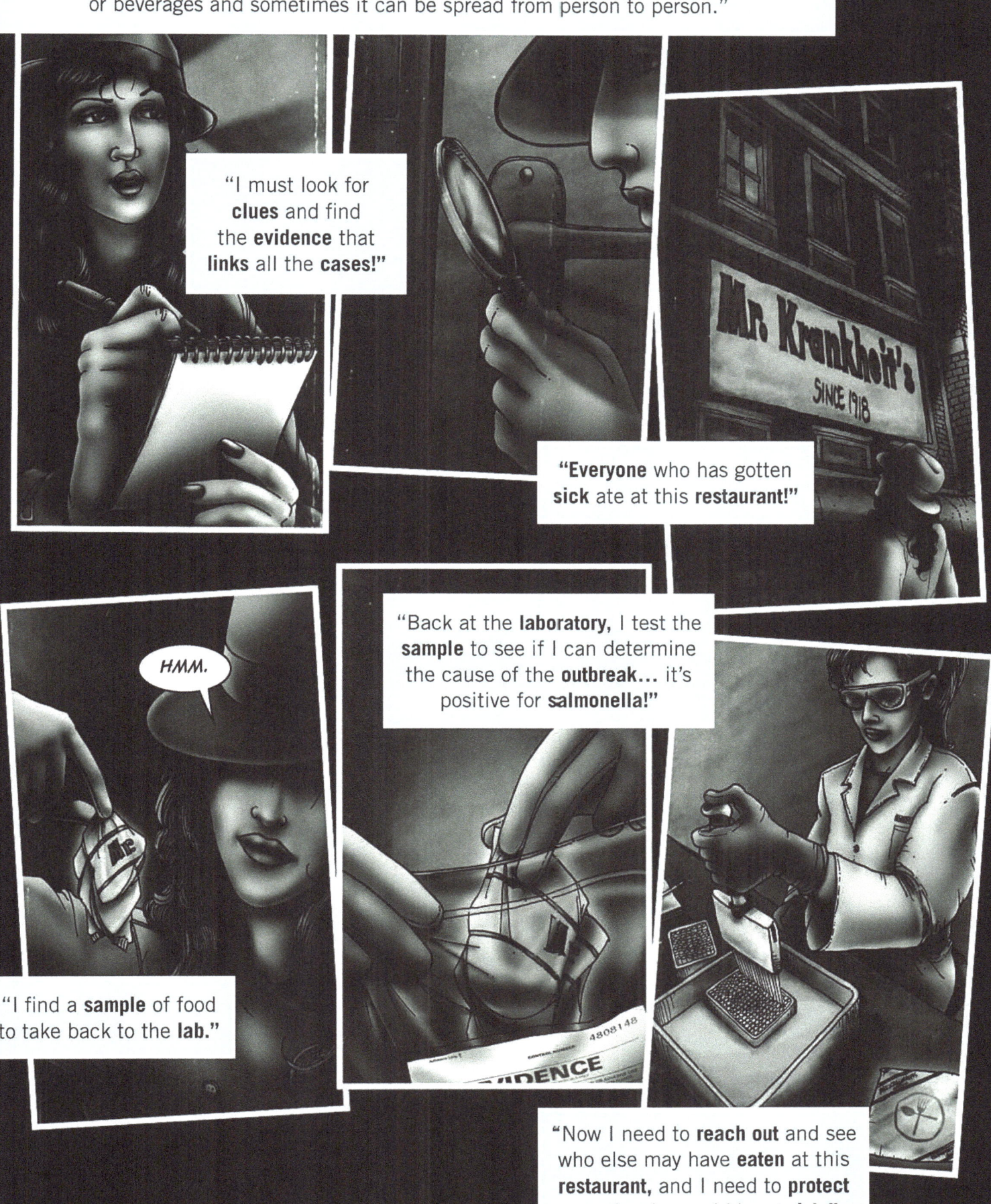

"There has been an **outbreak** of **foodborne illness.** I have been doing some studying prior to **CDC camp,** so I know that foodborne illness is caused by consuming **contaminated** food or beverages and sometimes it can be spread from person to person."

"I must look for **clues** and find the **evidence** that **links** all the **cases!**"

"**Everyone** who has gotten **sick** ate at this **restaurant!**"

HMM.

"I find a **sample** of food to take back to the **lab.**"

"Back at the **laboratory,** I test the **sample** to see if I can determine the cause of the **outbreak...** it's positive for **salmonella!**"

"Now I need to **reach out** and see who else may have **eaten** at this **restaurant,** and I need to **protect** people who could be at **risk.**"

4

2

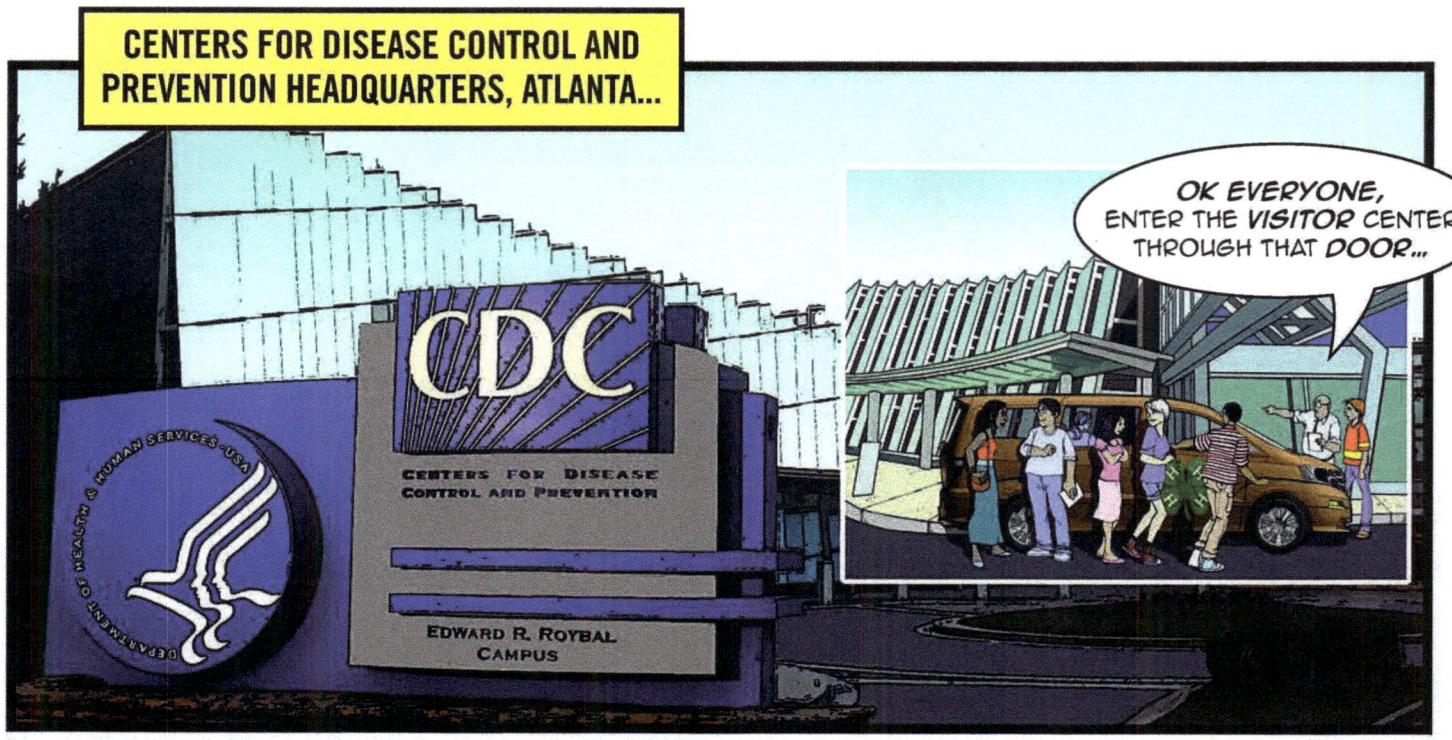

OK EVERYONE, ENTER THE *VISITOR* CENTER THROUGH THAT *DOOR*...

PLEASE *PICK* OUT YOUR *NAME TAG* AND *SIGN* NEXT TO YOUR *NAME* ON THE *LIST*...

I WISH *EDDIE* COULD'VE COME. *HE* WAS REALLY LOOKING *FORWARD* TO THIS...

VISITOR
Eddie Schwartz
NO. 207
EXPIRES: 10

YOU THINK *HE'S* STILL *SICK* FROM *FRIDAY*?

DISEASE detectives

2.

WHAT IS PUBLIC HEALTH?

NEXT, I'D LIKE TO TELL YOU HOW WE AT *CDC* FIGHT DISEASE.

CDC FOCUSES ON *PUBLIC HEALTH*, PROTECTING THE HEALTH AND SAFETY OF *GROUPS* OF PEOPLE.

PUBLIC HEALTH WORKERS
- Community Health
- Focus on Preventing Diseases
- Investigate Diseases in Groups of People

CLINICIANS
- Individual Health
- Focus on Treating Diseases
- Diagnose and Treat Disease in One Patient

I SURE HOPE EDDIE IS *FEELING* BETTER.

BACK AT EDDIE'S HOUSE...

MOM, I FEEL *WORSE.*

I'M TAKING YOU TO THE *DOCTOR.*

LATER THAT AFTERNOON...

36

2

WE'RE ALL *SO WORRIED* ABOUT EDDIE!

THANK YOU, SWEETHEART. EDDIE NEEDS *ALL* OF OUR LOVE AND SUPPORT RIGHT NOW.

HELLO, MRS. SCHWARTZ. I WOULD LIKE TO *SPEAK* TO YOU ABOUT EDDIE'S CONDITION, PLEASE COME WITH ME.

LET'S THINK BACK AND SEE IF WE CAN USE WHAT WE LEARNED AT *CDC DISEASE DETECTIVE CAMP* TO TRY AND SOLVE HOW EDDIE GOT SICK.

YEAH, *LET'S DO IT!* I THINK WE CAN AT LEAST ATTEMPT TO NARROW DOWN THE SOURCE OF HIS ILLNESS.

4

I WAS THINKING BACK TO BEFORE THE FAIR.

"I REMEMBER WALKING WITH EDDIE."

HE WAS TELLING ME ABOUT HIS PLANS TO SHOW HIS PIG, *HAMLET.* EDDIE SEEMED HEALTHY *THEN.*

YEAH, I'M THINKING BACK TO FRIDAY WHEN WE WERE ALL AT THE FAIR.

"I remember we all had **eaten together** at the snack bar. I had a soda, and you and Eddie got ice cream."

"Well, I think we can rule out ice cream because I had it too and **didn't get sick**."

SO FROSTY *DELICIOUS.*

SLURP

OW!

HANDS OFF!

SMACK!

3

KRIS: "Yeah, he was the only one of us to eat a **burrito**."

R.J.: "Yeah, I was **doubling down** on corn dogs, but I didn't get sick."

I'M GOING TO SIT DOWN WITH SOME OF THE *EPIDEMIOLOGISTS* HERE TO SEE IF THERE HAS BEEN AN *INCREASE IN RESPIRATORY ILLNESS* REPORTED IN THE AREA.

WE NEED TO ENSURE THIS NEW VIRUS IS NOT *SPREADING IN THE COMMUNITY.*

GOOD PLAN. I'M GOING TO FINISH GETTING SET UP HERE, AND THEN I'LL CHECK IN WITH ALISON TO SEE IF SHE HAS ANY *LEADS* TO FOLLOW UP ON.

HEY, DR. ALISON!

OH, *HI!* THIS IS QUITE A *COINCIDENCE.* WHAT BRINGS YOU HERE?

ALISON!

WE ARE HERE TO SEE OUR FRIEND, EDDIE, WHO IS IN THE *ICU.*

HE GOT SICK AT THE THOMAS COUNTY FAIR THE FRIDAY BEFORE OUR *CDC* FIELD TRIP.

WE WERE JUST USING WHAT WE LEARNED AT *CDC* TO TRY AND FIGURE OUT HOW HE GOT *SICK.*

HMMM... YOU ALL MIGHT BE ABLE TO *HELP* ME. IN FACT, *YOU ALREADY HAVE.*

I NEED TO SPEAK TO EDDIE'S MOM AND DOCTOR FIRST, BUT AFTER I'M FINISHED, *LET'S TALK.*

HI, MRS. SCHWARTZ, DR. ROSENBERG.

I'M DR. ALISON CROMWELL WITH *CDC* IN ATLANTA. I'D LIKE TO ASK YOU A FEW QUESTIONS ABOUT EDDIE'S ILLNESS...

DR. ROSENBERG.

CAN YOU TELL ME ABOUT EDDIE'S CONDITION AND WOULD YOU MIND IF I REVIEW HIS MEDICAL CHART?

MINUTES LATER...

3

ALEX, IT'S ALISON. I JUST TALKED TO EDDIE'S FRIENDS AGAIN. THEY SAID HE SHOWED A *PIG* AT THE FAIR.

INTERESTING... I JUST GOT OFF THE PHONE WITH THE *FAIR ORGANIZER.* WE'RE SUPPOSED TO MEET AT THE FAIRGROUNDS TO TALK. I'LL SEE IF HE CAN HAVE THE *FAIR VETERINARIAN* MEET US AS WELL.

SEVERAL HOURS LATER...

THANKS TO YOU BOTH FOR MEETING WITH ME.

DR. TOLANI, I UNDERSTAND THAT YOU ARE THE *VETERINARIAN* WHO INSPECTED THE ANIMALS AT THE FAIR.

CAN YOU TELL ME IF THERE WAS ANY *ILLNESS* AMONG THE ANIMALS?

2

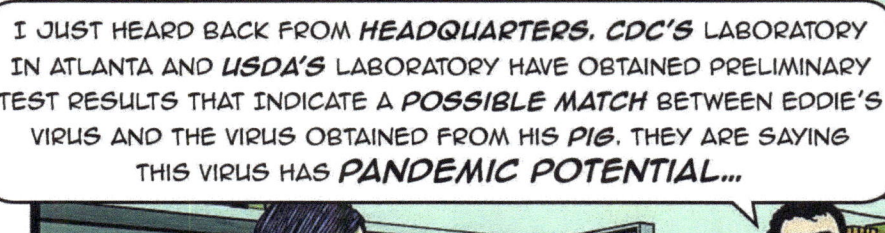

I JUST HEARD BACK FROM *HEADQUARTERS*. *CDC'S* LABORATORY IN ATLANTA AND *USDA'S* LABORATORY HAVE OBTAINED PRELIMINARY TEST RESULTS THAT INDICATE A *POSSIBLE MATCH* BETWEEN EDDIE'S VIRUS AND THE VIRUS OBTAINED FROM HIS *PIG*. THEY ARE SAYING THIS VIRUS HAS *PANDEMIC POTENTIAL*...

FOR A VIRUS TO CAUSE A *PANDEMIC,* THE MAJORITY OF THE WORLD'S POPULATION MUST *NOT HAVE EXISTING IMMUNITY* AGAINST IT, AND THE VIRUS MUST BE CAPABLE OF *SPREADING EASILY AND SUSTAINABLY FROM PERSON TO PERSON.*

YES. LET'S HOPE THAT THIS VIRUS ISN'T SPREADING FROM *PERSON TO PERSON* YET, BUT THAT'S WHAT WE *NEED* TO FIND OUT. LOCAL *HOSPITALS* AND *HEALTH CARE PROVIDERS* ARE STILL REPORTING *NORMAL PATTERNS OF ILLNESS,* ACCORDING TO OUR *STATE PUBLIC HEALTH COLLEAGUES.*

THE *FAIR MANAGER* SAID SOME PEOPLE REPORTED GETTING *SICK* FOLLOWING THE FAIR, AND HE ALSO SAID MORE *PIGS* HAVE TESTED POSITIVE.

NOPE, WE'RE JUST GETTING STARTED...

OKAY. LOOKS LIKE OUR JOB *ISN'T OVER.*

YES, WE WILL NEED TO FOLLOW UP WITH HIM AND OUR *STATE PUBLIC HEALTH PARTNERS* TO SEE IF WE CAN LEARN MORE ABOUT THEIR ILLNESS AND POSSIBLY GET THOSE PEOPLE *TESTED.* LET'S GO AHEAD AND ALSO *COORDINATE* WITH THE *STATE PUBLIC HEALTH DEPARTMENT* AND *HEALTH CARE PROVIDERS.* WE CAN ASK THEM TO TAKE SAMPLES FOR *TESTING* FROM ANY PATIENTS WITH *FLU-LIKE ILLNESS* THAT HAVE HAD RECENT *CONTACT WITH PIGS.* WE SHOULD ALSO SET UP A PHONE CALL WITH *STATE* AND *FEDERAL ANIMAL HEALTH OFFICIALS.*

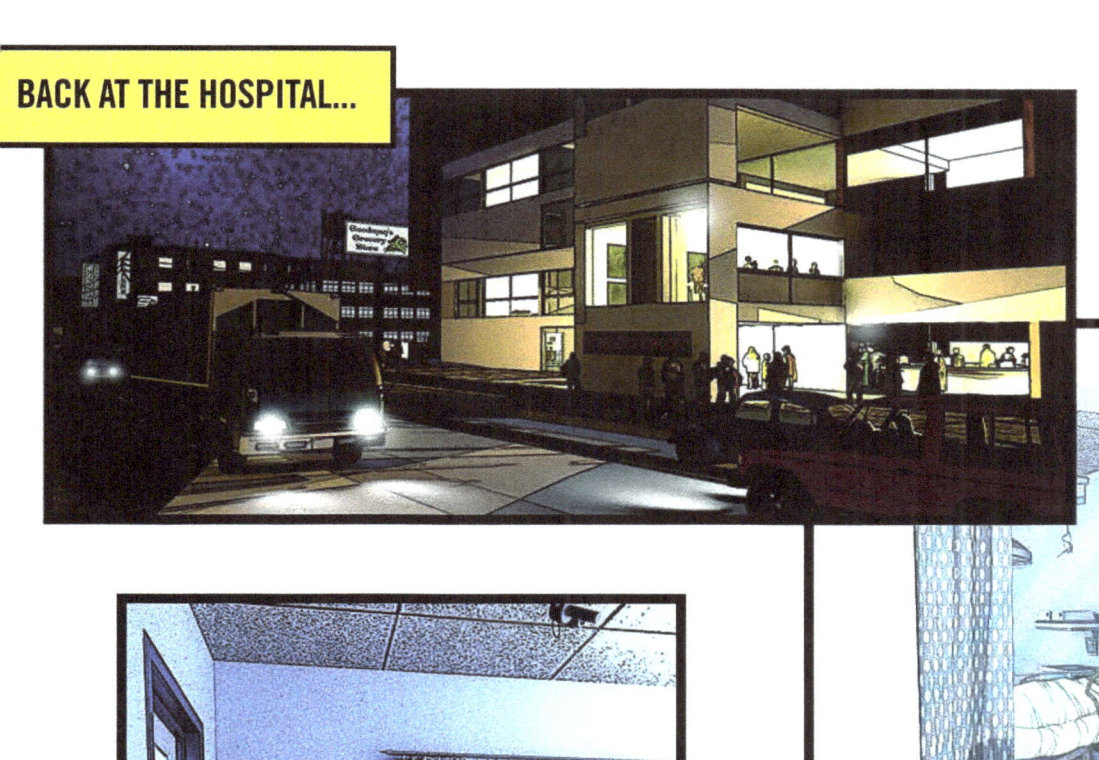

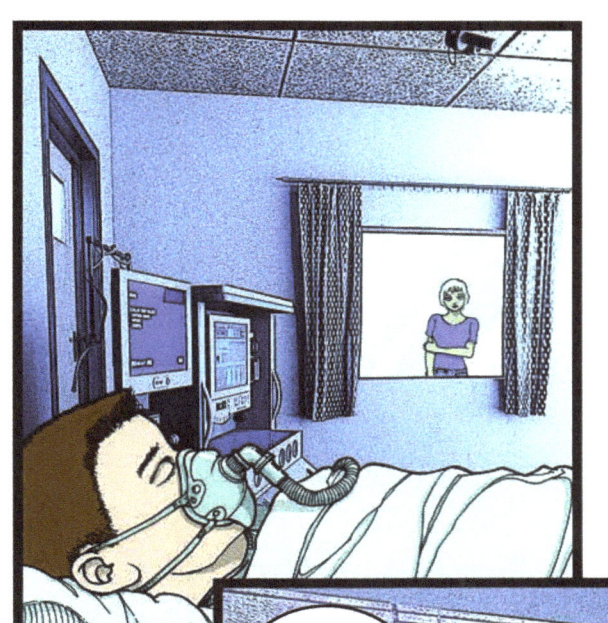

KEEP *FIGHTING*, EDDIE...

I'M *HERE* FOR YOU.

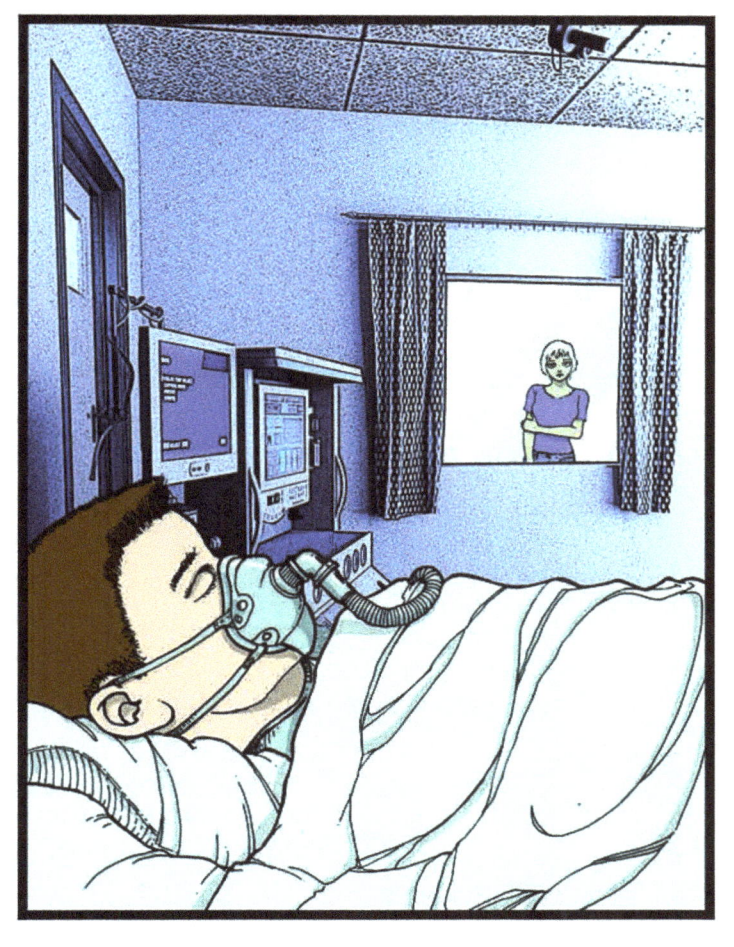

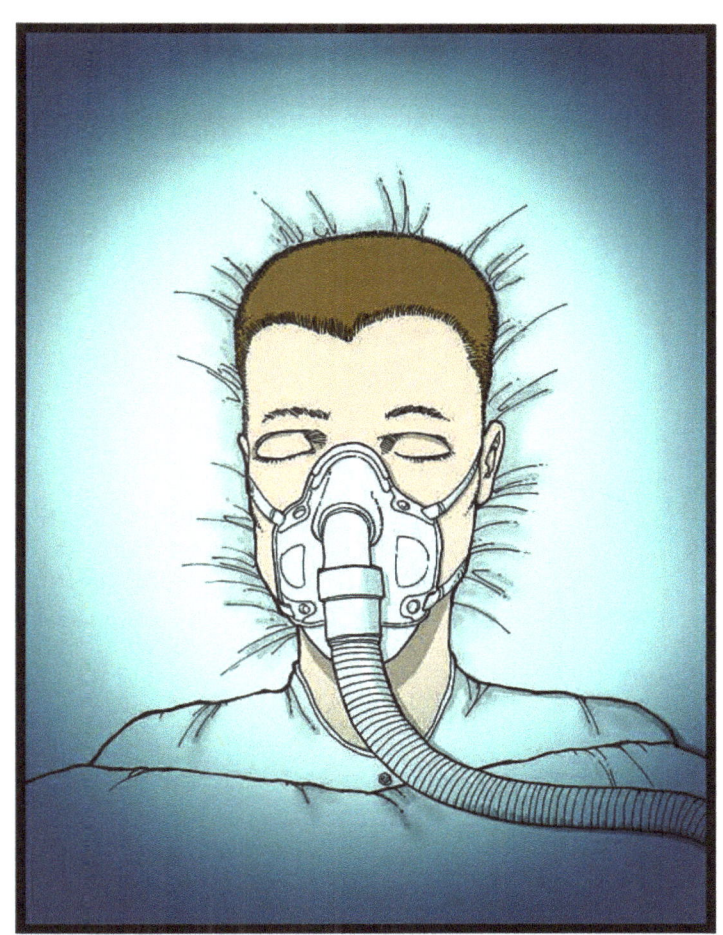

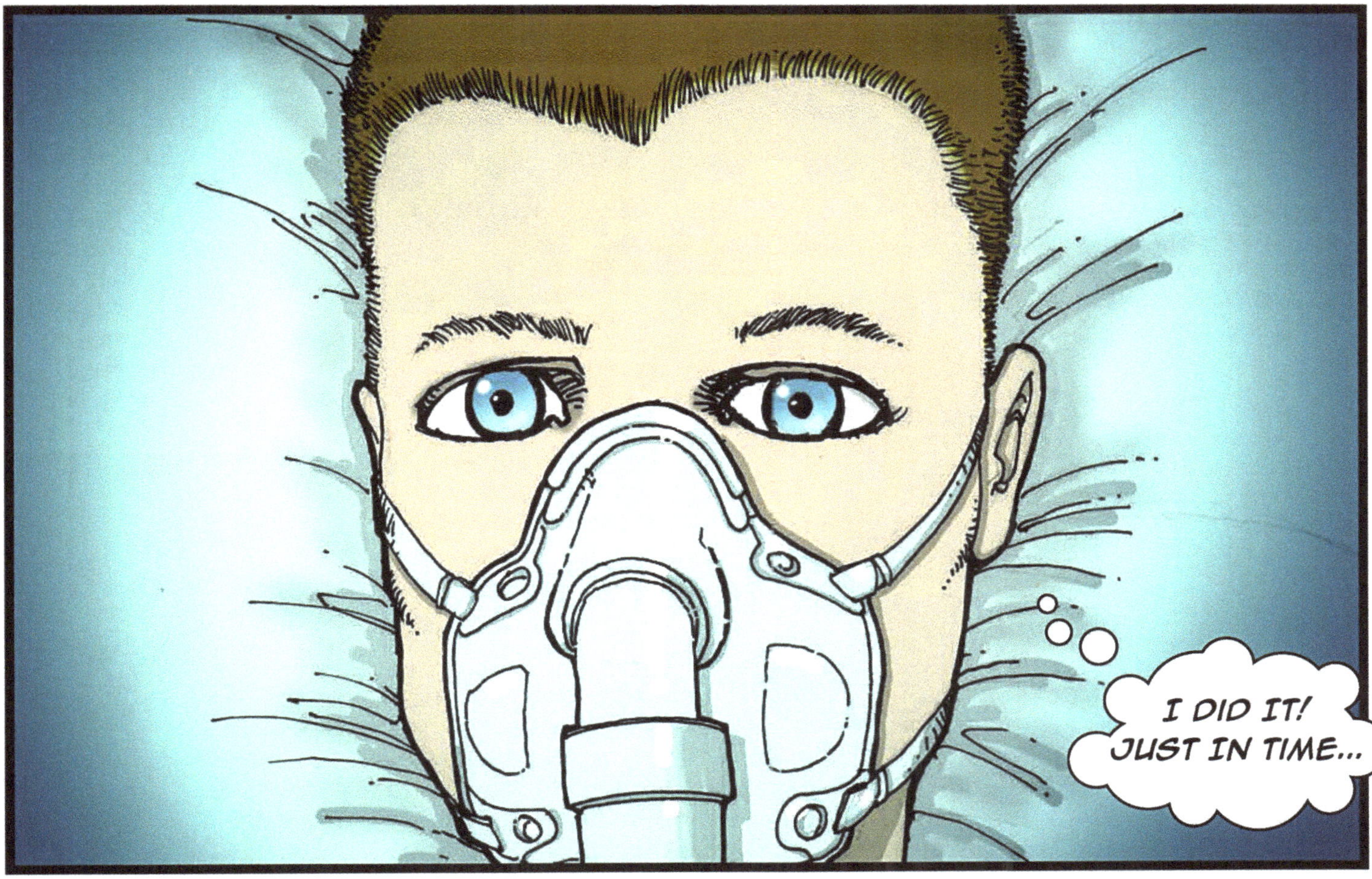

I DID IT! JUST IN TIME...

OH, I SEE. THAT MAKES SENSE. BUT HOW DO PEOPLE *KNOW* IF THEY ARE AT HIGH RISK?

ALISON SAID TO CHECK *CDC'S FLU WEBSITE* IF WE HAD ANY QUESTIONS.

I REMEMBER HER SAYING THAT IN ADDITION TO PEOPLE WITH *ASTHMA*, PEOPLE AT HIGH RISK INCLUDED KIDS *YOUNGER THAN 5* YEARS OLD, *PREGNANT WOMEN*, AND PEOPLE WITH OTHER *LONG TERM HEALTH CONDITIONS*, LIKE DIABETES, TO NAME A FEW.

THAT'S GOOD TO KNOW. SO IS THERE ANYTHING ELSE THEY *RECOMMEND* DOING TO *PREVENT GETTING SICK* WITH ONE OF THESE VIRUSES?

WELL, THE EIS OFFICERS SAID THAT *PIGS* DON'T ALWAYS *APPEAR SICK* WHEN THEY HAVE THE *FLU*, SO *WASHING YOUR HANDS* BEFORE AND AFTER HANDLING THEM IS A *GOOD IDEA*.

THEY ALSO SAID YOU SHOULDN'T *EAT* OR PUT ANYTHING IN YOUR *MOUTH* WHEN AROUND PIGS. THIS DOESN'T REALLY APPLY TO ANY OF US, BUT THEY ALSO SAID *NOT* TO BRING ANY KIDS' TOYS, PACIFIERS AND STROLLERS INTO *ANIMAL AREAS* AT FAIRS.

AH! I SEE. DR. TOLANI THE *FAIR VETERINARIAN* TOLD ME THAT THEY TAKE PRECAUTIONS ON THE *ANIMAL HEALTH* SIDE, AS WELL.

SHE SAID IT TAKES EVERYONE WORKING TOGETHER TO *KEEP ANIMALS* AND *PEOPLE HEALTHY*.

THAT'S WHY THERE ARE *SO MANY RULES* WE FOLLOW WHEN WE RAISE AND SHOW OUR ANIMALS, SUCH AS NOT KEEPING THE PIGS AT THE FAIR LONGER THAN *THREE DAYS*.

SHE SAID THAT HELPS *REDUCE SPREAD OF DISEASE* AMONG PIGS AND PEOPLE.

WHILE EDDIE WAS IN THE *HOSPITAL*, ALISON TOLD ME A FEW MORE THINGS.

SHE SAID WHEN *FLU VIRUSES* FROM *PIGS* INFECT *PEOPLE*, IT'S CALLED A *"VARIANT FLU VIRUS"* INFECTION.

SHE SAID VARIANT VIRUS INFECTIONS DON'T HAPPEN OFTEN, BUT SOME OCCUR *EVERY YEAR*, PARTICULARLY DURING FAIR SEASON.

ALISON ALSO SAID THAT VARIANT VIRUSES ARE *DIFFERENT* FROM THE FLU VIRUSES THAT NORMALLY MAKE PEOPLE SICK DURING THE FLU SEASON. SINCE PEOPLE AREN'T OFTEN *EXPOSED* TO VIRUSES FROM *PIGS*, MOST *DON'T HAVE ANTIBODIES* THAT PROTECT AGAINST VARIANT VIRUSES.

AS WE LEARNED DURING *DISEASE DETECTIVE CAMP*, OUR BODIES' *IMMUNE SYSTEM* PRODUCES ANTIBODIES TO FIGHT AGAINST INFECTION, AND THE *SAFEST* WAY TO GET ANTIBODIES IS THROUGH *VACCINATION*. ALTHOUGH THE FLU VACCINE ISN'T DESIGNED TO PROTECT AGAINST *VARIANT FLU*, IT IS STILL *IMPORTANT* TO GET, BECAUSE IT CAN HELP *PROTECT* US FROM GETTING THE FLU AND SPREADING IT TO OTHERS, INCLUDING *HAMLET*.

OH *WOW!* HOW OFTEN DO PEOPLE GET REALLY *SICK* FROM THESE VIRUSES, LIKE I DID?

NOT TOO OFTEN. ALISON SAID THAT *MOST* PEOPLE WITH *VARIANT FLU* JUST HAVE *TYPICAL* FLU ILLNESS, BUT JUST AS WITH ANY TYPE OF FLU, SOME PEOPLE WILL GET *REALLY SICK* FROM VARIANT FLU. THIS IS PARTICULARLY IMPORTANT FOR PEOPLE AT *HIGH RISK*, LIKE YOU.

YEAH, ALISON SAID THAT *ANY FLU VIRUS* INFECTION CAN BE *DANGEROUS*, EVEN DEADLY, EVEN FOR OTHERWISE *HEALTHY* PEOPLE.

SHE SAID *CDC* WAS INVESTIGATING TO SEE IF THE VIRUS YOU HAD IS *SPREADING BETWEEN PEOPLE...*

ON THAT POINT, ALISON SAID THAT THEY **ALWAYS** TRY TO INVESTIGATE VARIANT VIRUS INFECTIONS TO SEE IF THEY ARE SPREADING FROM PERSON-TO-PERSON.

SHE SAID **MOST** VARIANT VIRUSES SPREAD FROM AN **INFECTED PIG** TO A **PERSON**, BUT THESE VIRUSES USUALLY ARE **NOT ABLE** TO SPREAD EASILY FROM PERSON TO PERSON, LIKE **SEASONAL FLU.**

OH, YEAH! WHEN A FLU VIRUS FROM **ANIMALS** GAINS THE ABILITY TO SPREAD EASILY FROM **PERSON TO PERSON**, THAT'S WHEN A **PANDEMIC** CAN OCCUR.

IN FACT, THAT'S HOW THE **2009 FLU PANDEMIC** OCCURRED. ALEX TOLD ME THE 2009 **H1N1 VIRUS** HAD A MIX OF GENES FROM **NORTH AMERICAN PIGS, PIGS FROM EUROPE AND ASIA, BIRDS, AND EVEN HUMANS.**

THAT'S... **KIND OF CRAZY!**

WOW! YOU GUYS JUST TAUGHT ME **A LOT!**

ADDENDUM

Please visit the following websites for additional information about health topics and recommendations discussed in The Junior Disease Detectives: Operation Outbreak.

CDC WEBSITE RESOURCES:

CDC Flu Website: https://www.cdc.gov/flu/

CDC Swine/Variant Flu Website: https://www.cdc.gov/flu/swineflu/index.htm

What People Who Raise Pigs Need to Know About Influenza (Flu):
https://www.cdc.gov/flu/swineflu/people-raise-pigs-flu.htm

Key Facts about Human Infections with Variant Viruses:
https://www.cdc.gov/flu/swineflu/keyfacts-variant.htm

Key Facts about Swine Influenza in Pigs:
https://www.cdc.gov/flu/swineflu/keyfacts_pigs.htm

Key Facts for People Exhibiting Pigs at Fairs:
https://www.cdc.gov/flu/pdf/swineflu/fair_exhibitor_factsheet.pdf

Take Action to Prevent the Spread of Flu Between Pigs and People:
https://www.cdc.gov/flu/pdf/swineflu/prevent-spread-flu-pigs-at-fairs.pdf

CDC Healthy Pets Healthy People Website: https://www.cdc.gov/healthypets/index.html

CDC Zoonotic Diseases Website: https://www.cdc.gov/onehealth/basics/zoonotic-diseases.html

CDC Pandemic Flu Website: https://www.cdc.gov/flu/pandemic-resources/index.htm

USDA WEBSITE RESOURCES:

Zoonotic Influenza and Measures for Prevention at Fairs:
http:/nasphv.org/documentsCompendiaZoonoticInfluenza.html

Influenza in Swine: https://www.usda.gov/topics/animals/one-health/influenza-swine

USDA Surveillance for Influenza A Virus in Swine Update:
https://www.aphis.usda.gov/aphis/ourfocus/animalhealth/sa_animal_disease_information/sa_swine_health/ct_siv_surveillance/

Acknowledgments

4-H, NIFA, USDA Subject Matter Experts and Contributors

Lisa Lauxman, Ph.D.   Amy McCune, Ph.D.

USDA-APHIS Subject Matter Experts and Contributors

Tracey Dutcher, DVM   Tom Gomez, DVM

Ellen Kasari, DVM

CDC Subject Matter Experts and Contributors

Alicia Budd, MPH   Erin Burns, MA

Emily Eisenberg Lobelo, MS   Joe Gregg, MA

Dan Jernigan, MD, MPH   Michael Jhung, MD, MPH

James Kile, DVM, MPH   Lisa Koonin, DrPH, MN, MPH

Josh Mott, Ph.D.   Sonja Olsen, Ph.D.

Lexi Sowers, MA   Jerry Tokars, MD, MPH

Sue Trock, DVM, MPH   Abbey Wojno, Ph.D.

Special thanks to Tolani Francisco, DVM, MPH

One way to think about how living things get sick is to imagine a triangle.

The three corners represent the **environment**...

...the **host**...

...and the cause of the disease, the **Agent**.

All three aspects of this triangle must come together for disease to occur. Disease agents can be **non-infectious** or **infectious**.

Non-infectious agents are non-living things that are toxic to the host, like radiation or chemicals...

...while infectious agents are **organisms** that invade a host to survive.

Only infectious agents can spread, or **transmit**, between hosts.

Infectious disease agents, otherwise known as pathogens, must infect a host in order to grow, or **replicate**.

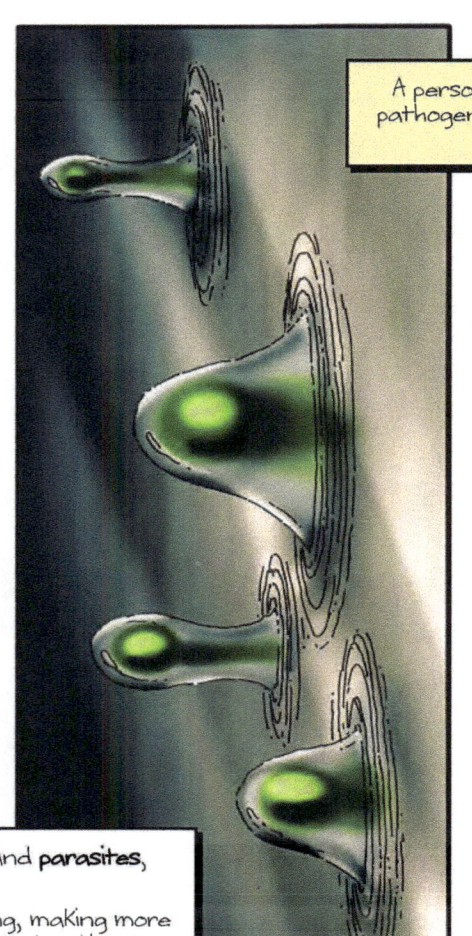

A person can become infected with a pathogen when in the same environment as the agent...

Human pathogens, like **viruses**, **bacteria**, and **parasites**, evolved to infect people.

Their survival is dependent on quickly invading, making more of themselves, and efficiently transmitting to others.

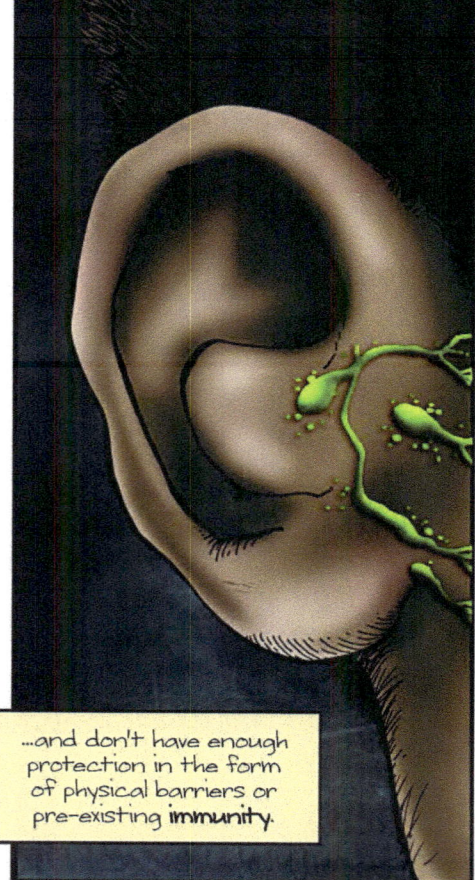

...and don't have enough protection in the form of physical barriers or pre-existing **immunity**.

If a pathogen gets past a host's defenses, it will attempt to infect the host and begin replicating itself.

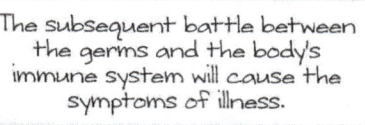

The subsequent battle between the germs and the body's immune system will cause the symptoms of illness.

Many cells will be destroyed as germs kill them through replicating and as collateral damage from the activated immune cells.

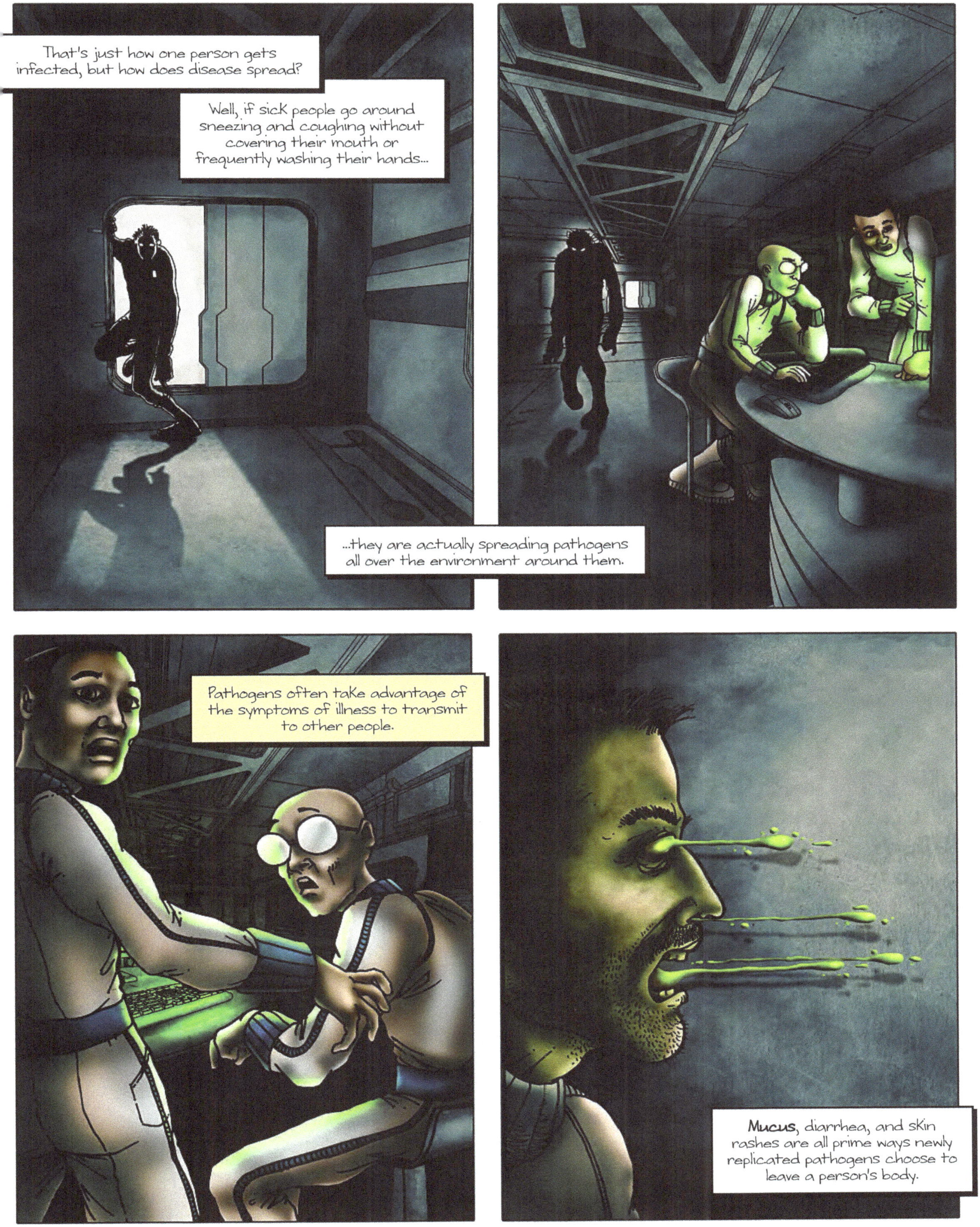

That's just how one person gets infected, but how does disease spread?

Well, if sick people go around sneezing and coughing without covering their mouth or frequently washing their hands...

...they are actually spreading pathogens all over the environment around them.

Pathogens often take advantage of the symptoms of illness to transmit to other people.

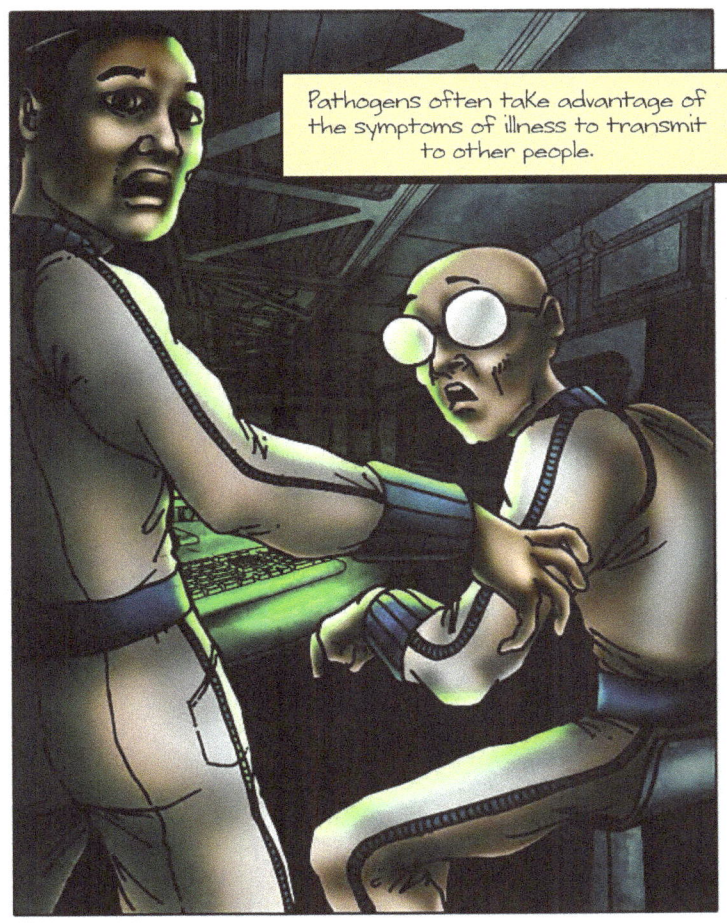

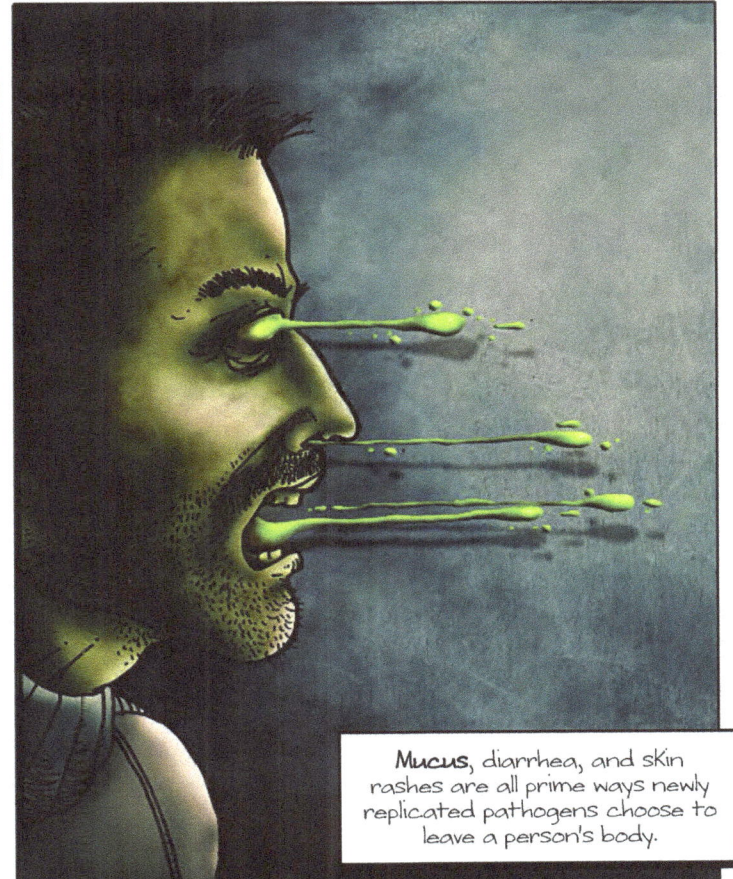

Mucus, diarrhea, and skin rashes are all prime ways newly replicated pathogens choose to leave a person's body.

One person can infect many more people.

This is how infectious disease outbreaks can begin.

Now, what if **YOU** come along to the environment as an unsuspecting host?

Because of this, you should be aware of others with symptoms of illness around you.

If you are in a contaminated environment and don't take the proper precautions, you can get sick, too!

Encourage your friends and family to stay home when they are sick and to see a doctor if their symptoms persist.

To protect yourself every day, get in the habit of washing your hands, getting plenty of rest and exercise, and eating a balanced diet...

... and avoiding close contact with contagious, **acutely ill** people whenever possible.

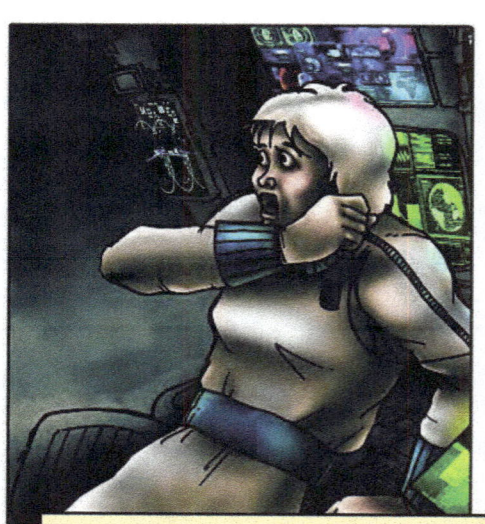

If **you** want to study how germs work, how pathogens spread from person to person, and how to make new drugs to fight disease, you could work at the CDC as a microbiologist!

WORD	DEFINITION
agent	the cause of a disease
bacteria	a member of a large group of single cellular microorganisms that have cell walls but lack organelles and an organized nucleus, including some that can cause disease
environment	the surroundings or conditions in which a person or organism exists
host	a person or organism on or in which another organism lives
immunity	the ability of an organism to resist a particular infection or toxin by the action of specific antibodies or sensitized white blood cells
infectious	the ability of a living organism to transmit to people or other organisms through the environment
mucus	a slimy substance secreted by mucous membranes and glands for lubrication and protection from infection
non-infectious agent	non-living things that are toxic to the host but are not transmitted through the environment, like radiation or chemicals
organism	an individual life form
parasite	an organism that lives in or on another organism (its host) and benefits by deriving nutrients at the host's expense
pathogen	a bacterium, virus, or other microorganism that can cause disease in humans, animals, or plants
replicate	make an exact copy of; reproduce
transmit	the ability to pass on from one place or person to another
virus	an infective agent that typically consists of a nucleic acid molecule in a protein coat, is too small to be seen by light microscopy, and is able to multiply only within the living cells of a host

Written by Dr. Victoria Jeisy-Scott
Penciled and Inked by Bob Hobbs
Digital Color and Lettering by Kristen Immoor (Contractor)

This project was a collaboration between the Office of the Associate Director for Communication, the Office of the
Associate Director for Laboratory Science and Safety, and the National Center for Chronic Disease Prevention and Health Promotion,
Division of Population Health, School Health Branch

**U.S. Department of
Health and Human Services**
Centers for Disease
Control and Prevention

CS238388

Ask a Scientist

How Does My Body Fight Disease?

In general, your body fights disease by keeping things out of your body that are foreign.

Your primary defense against pathogenic germs are physical barriers like your skin.

You also produce **pathogen**-destroying chemicals, like **lysozyme**, found on parts of your body without skin, including your tears and **mucus membranes**.

A group of **innate immune system** cells will be there to capture and destroy the invading germ.

These cells are always on alert for germs, patrolling your body like soldiers looking for invaders.

These innate cells then communicate to the rest of your body regarding the problem by activating the **inflammatory response**.

The swelling, pain and higher temperature caused by inflammation attracts more cells to the site of infection.

The innate cells also scout out information for another, more specific group of cells called the **adaptive immune system** cells.

The innate immune cells train the **adaptive immune cells** to fight disease in two ways.

First, they instruct the adaptive immune cells how to respond to the invader by releasing chemicals called **cytokines**.

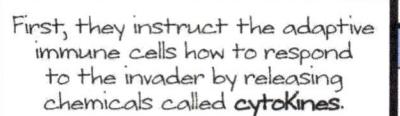

CytoKines are signals recognized by cells, telling them what to do and where to go. Your body responds to threats in different ways depending on the cytoKine signal released by your immune cells.

Second, the innate antigen presenting cells capture and break down the invaders into pieces that can be recognized by the adaptive immune system, called **antigens**.

Every invader's antigenic pattern is unique.

Together, cytoKines and antigens train individual adaptive immune cells to recognize and destroy specific patterns of each foreign invader.

The next time that this pathogen tries to infect you...

Your adaptive immune cells will remember it!

Your body will be better trained and ready to stop the threat before it makes you sick.

Working together, the innate and the adaptive cells of your immune system have the ability to protect you from nearly anything trying to invade your body.

But this is war. It's not that easy! Some pathogens, including those that cause flu, strep throat, and malaria, can mutate and change the way they look to your immune system over time.

They disguise themselves by changing their surface antigens in a process called **antigenic variation**.

This disguise makes it harder for your immune system to recognize them.

Because it's harder to recognize the mutated germs, your body's immune system has a harder time protecting you from them, even though you've been exposed to them before.

This is why you can get sick from flu and strep throat multiple times.

For these type of germs, just because you've been sick once, doesn't mean you won't get sick again. Every year has the potential to produce new disguised germs that can make you sick.

But there's some good news! You can help your body prepare and defend itself against pathogens and disease by getting your regular vaccinations, including the one for flu.

WE'VE CAUGHT ONE, SIR!

Vaccines are made up of small, harmless pieces of the pathogen you are trying to protect yourself against.

Antigen Presenting Cells give the antigen from the vaccine to the adaptive immune cells.

WORD	DEFINITION
adaptive immune system	The immune response that targets specific foreign invaders. It is also responsible for immunological memory, leading to enhanced immune response to subsequent encounters with that foreign antigen.
antibody	A protein secreted by B-cells that identify and neutralize foreign antigens. These proteins can be secreted and circulate in your blood for many years after being exposed to a pathogen or vaccine to protect you from re-infection from that same invader.
antigen	Any of various substances that, when introduced into a living body, causes the production of antibodies.
antigen presenting cells (APC)	Innate immune cells that capture, process and present foreign antigens to activate an adaptive immune response to specifically target that threat.
antigenic variation	The method a germ uses to alter its surface proteins in order to evade a host immune response. This allows pathogens to cause re-infection, as their antigens are no longer recognized by the host's immune system.
B-cell (B)	An adaptive immune cell that monitors for the presence of foreign antigens outside of a person's cells. When activated, they will secrete antibodies to specifically recognize surface antigens on an invading germ or foreign molecule, marking them for destruction by the innate immune system.
cytokines	Any of various molecules secreted by immune cells that carry signals to and have an effect on neighboring cells.
immune system	The bodily system of organs, tissues, cells, and cell products, which protects the body by detecting the presence of, and disabling, disease-causing agents in the body.
immunologist	A scientist who studies how an organism defends itself against pathogens and other foreign invaders to the body.
inflammatory response	The way in which an organism protects itself from harmful stimulation, such as germs, injury or irritants. The function of inflammation is to eliminate the initial cause of cell injury, clear out dead cells and tissues damaged from the original injury, and activate the immune system to initiate tissue repair.
innate immune system	The immune response that provides immediate, but non-specific defense against foreign invaders. It is primarily responsible for initiating the overall immune response and activating the adaptive immune response.
lymphoid tissue	The location for production and maturation of the adaptive immune cells. The lymphatic system is part of the circulatory system, constantly screening an organisms blood for foreign invaders. Major lymphoid organs include the lymph nodes, spleen and thymus.
lysozyme	A molecule made by a person's body that destroys pathogens, found in tears and mucus.
mucous membrane	A lubricating barrier that lines various surfaces or organs, as of the respiratory, digestive, and genitourinary tracts.
mucus	A slimy, slightly sticky material that coats and protects certain parts of the body, such as the inside of the nose and throat.
pathogen	Any organism that causes disease, such as a bacterium, virus, parasite, or fungus.
polymorphonuclear leukocytes (PMN)	Also known as granulocytes, are found in the bloodstream and are usually the first to arrive to an infection or injured site. They amplify the ongoing inflammatory response by releasing more cytokines, eat and destroy invading germs in the affected area.
T-cell (T)	An adaptive immune cell that monitors for the presence of foreign antigens presented to them from inside the organism's cells. When activated, they can direct the ongoing immune response through secreting a variety of cytokines or can directly kill the infected cells.
vaccine	Pieces of germs causing disease that are dead or not active. Vaccines are used to help the immune system protect against the disease.

Written by Dr. Victoria Jeisy-Scott
Penciled and Inked by Bob Hobbs
Digital Color and Lettering by Kristen Immoor (Contractor)

This project was a collaboration between the Office of the Associate Director for Communication, the Office of the
Associate Director for Laboratory Science and Safety, and the National Center for Chronic Disease Prevention and Health Promotion,
Division of Population Health, School Health Branch

**U.S. Department of
Health and Human Services**
Centers for Disease
Control and Prevention

CS238388

www.ingramcontent.com/pod-product-compliance
Lightning Source LLC
Chambersburg PA
CBHW041555240626
47164CB00012B/210